SOLAR
PUNKS

T0348800

GUME LAUREL III

WEST **44** BOOKS™

**Please visit our website, www.west44books.com.
For a free color catalog of all our high-quality books,
call toll free 1-800-398-2504.**

Cataloging-in-Publication Data

Names: Laurel, Gume.
Title: Solar punks / Gume Laurel III.
Description: Buffalo, NY : West 44, 2025. | Series: West 44
YA verse
Identifiers: ISBN 9781978597631 (pbk.) | ISBN
9781978597624 (library bound) | ISBN 9781978597648
(ebook)
Subjects: LCSH: Secrecy--Fiction. | Communities--Fiction.
| Sustainable development--Fiction. | Interpersonal
relations--Fiction. | Island life--Fiction.
Classification: LCC PZ7.1.L387 So 2025 | DDC [F]--dc23

First Edition

Published in 2025 by
Enslow Publishing LLC
2544 Clinton Street
Buffalo, New York 14224

Editor: Caitie McAneney
Designer: Tanya Dellaccio Keeney

Photo Credits: photopixel/Shutterstock.com.

Printed in the United States of America

CPSIA compliance information: Batch #CW25W44: For further information contact
Enslow Publishing LLC at 1-800-398-2504.

Find us on

*Dedicated to my nieces and nephew,
and those who come after you.
For a cleaner, hopeful tomorrow.*

ISLA SOLA

Rolling blue waves.
Clear skies always.
Countless stars
twinkle at night.
Seagulls take flight.
Sandy shores
dressed in
seashells.

Families
living in
treehouses.

Running water
and electricity
powered by

waterwheels,
wind turbines,
solar panels.

Advanced
technology
in harmony
with nature.

Here at home

on

Isla Sola.

WE SKIPPED AFTERNOON CHORES

"Again, Veny?!"
Dad shouts
from the sand.

"One last wave!"
I yell from
my surfboard.
We're far
from shore.

Nano whines,
"Told you we'd get busted."
His thick, bronze body
lies over his surfboard.

Lupita sighs,
"Waves weren't
worth it, either."
Her hands cup
cold salt water
to pour over
her shaved head.

"This one's
promising."
I point my stubbly chin
at the wave rolling in.

GRITOS

We grip our
surfboards.
Feel the ocean
swell. Rise.

More.

And more

Like your
chest when
you take a
deep breath.

Until

the tide

lifts us

up high!

From
our bellies,

we shout

out

gritos.

WAVE HITS ITS PEAK

We pop up
on our surfboards.

Ride over
the ocean.

In the
space where

water,
air,
and sun meet.

We become
something like a

fish, bird,
and shooting star.

Like Mother Nature
looking in the mirror.

Streaks of
white sea-foam.
Splashing blue tide.
We cut through the waves
like a knife splitting butter.

We safely ride
onto the shore.

DAD'S EARS ARE MAROON

Not from
the sun.

"Get back
to the village,"
Dad growls at
Nano and Lupita.
"Before I decide
to tell your parents
about this."

They rush away
like crabs
dodging
pelicans.

I try to
scurry
close
behind
them.

Dad grabs
my forearm.

I'm caught
in his snare.

DAD SNATCHES MY SURFBOARD

"It's bad
enough
to skip
chores."
Dad's bushy, black mustache
becomes a dancing caterpillar
whenever he speaks.
"Convincing
others to do it, too?
That's as bad
as it gets."

       I frown and say,
       "Chores can
       be done later."

Dad huffs.
Turns away.
Swipes my
beige vest
off the ground.
Shakes out
the sand.

His anger
shows with
each harsh shake.

~~~

The
        sand
                blows
                        away,

                as if it
                        knows
                                it doesn't
                                        belong.

Dad tosses
me my vest.

Light. Silky.
Tougher than stone.
It protects skin from
harmful UV rays.
It's made of web
from the spider farm.

Everybody on
Isla Sola
wears one.

"Fix your hair
before we get back."
Dad heads for
the village.
"I don't want anyone to
notice you've selfishly
been out here."

ON THE WAY BACK TO THE VILLAGE

We pass by
dodo bird nests.

The dodos are
so used to me,
they let me
pet their heads.
Scratch their bellies.

All over
the ground
are white
feathers.
I pick out
the bushiest ones.
Stick them into
my curly, black
mohawk.

My own style.

MOM WATERS HER GOLDEN POTHOS VINES

They grow
from
hanging
glass pots
in the
living room.

The vines
stretch
down
to the
wooden
floor.

Their roots
press against
the inside
of the pot.
Ready
to escape.

Mom
sets down
her copper
watering can.

She sighs.
"*Mijo*, why did
you skip chores?"

～～～

"I hate
churning the
compost pile,"
I say.

I drop onto
the stiff beanbag
couch.

> Mom sits beside me.
> Her long black braids
> have palo santo and sage
> woven into them.
> She straightens
> my feathers
> and says,
> "You've skipped
> chores you love
> in the past, too."

"I don't
always feel
like doing
my chores."

> "It's not
> about
> what we
> feel like
> doing."

FOR THE
MILLIONTH TIME

Mom tells me,
"It's our responsibility
to do what's best for
the community."

"Even when
we don't want
to be responsible."
I groan the
second half
of the phrase.

Mom's walnut cheeks
flush to raspberry.
"*Especially*,"
she corrects me.
"*Especially* when
we don't want to
be responsible."

I know
the correct
phrase.
There's
no reason
why
I said it
wrong.

Maybe only to
poke the beehive.

REBEL WITHOUT A CAUSE

Mom tugs my ear.
"No son of mine
needs to act like
a punk."

"I'm your
only son."

"My miracle."

Her
miracle.

My
curse.

A subtle
reminder.

The family
bloodline
will end
with me.

MOM RUBS MY BACK

Mom says,
"You think
too loudly, Veny."

I say,
"It's not fair."

"I know."

"It's not
my fault
I'm the
odd-numbered
kid out of my
whole generation."

"I know."

"If there was
one more person
my age, I could
have a life partner.
I'd feel like a true
part of our community.
Not like a leftover piece
from a completed puzzle."

"I know, *mijo*."

MY WHITE CORAL NECKLACE

weighs
heavy
around
my neck.

Everyone on
Isla Sola

gets one
at birth.

When you
grow up, you
choose your
life partner.
You and your
life partner
exchange
white
coral
necklaces.

Mine
will
never
leave
my
neck.

MY EYES BURN LIKE FIRE

Tears
don't
fall

out.

I hold
them
in.

Like breath
underwater.

Like air
in lungs.

Like sky
holding
stars
scared
to fall

in

the

night.

COMMUNITY DINNER

Everyone
gathers on the
forest floor
at the
village center.
Beneath our
towering
treehouses
made of
reflective glass
solar panels.

Tonight, we eat
sunflower steak.
It's baked
to a crisp.
Jasmine rice
with basil.
Grapefruit
for dessert.

Coconut water
to wash it all down.

I could
drink it
by the barrel
if given
the chance.

AFTER DINNER

musicians play.
Guitars carved
from palm trees.
Rainsticks filled
with beetle shells.
Brass shofars.
Pan flutes.
Electric handpans.

Every adult
dances with glee.

Claps. Sways.
Like ocean waves.
Sings along, merrily.

> *El sol.*
> *El sol.*
> *Keeper of day.*

> *El sol.*
> *El sol.*
> *Giver and flame.*

WE TEENAGERS

pack in
tightly
beside the
bonfire.

We wait on
Elder Ernestina,

the oldest
member
of

The Council.

    The Council

    is in
    charge
    of

    Isla Sola.

    They make
    all the big
    decisions.

        Most of them
        are old enough
        to have
        seen
        it all.

ELDER ERNESTINA

wears a beige robe,
same as the rest of
The Council.

Except
hers is
special.

Her robes grow
orange hibiscus
for bees
to enjoy.

There's
always
buzzing
when
Ernestina's
nearby.

Her apprentice,
Isabella, is

Ernestina's
constant shadow.
Learning for the day
she replaces
Ernestina
on

The Council.

CAMPFIRE TALES

Ernestina
waves her
hands while
telling us
stories,
as if she's
sewing
her words
into the air.

"Isla Sola has
always been home.
Since the sun first
learned to shine.
We have always
lived on this island
without harming it.
We never take more
than we need.
Never treat
its water, air, and earth
as dull or lifeless.

Isla Sola is as alive
as you and me.
It is water, air, and earth.
We must always live in
harmony with Isla Sola.
With all living beings."

BEDTIME

Our community
never parties too late.
Every morning
is an early start.

I bundle up in
my bedroom
hammock.

Wind gusts through
my open window.
Rocks me
like a baby
in a cradle.

While asleep, my brain
does that annoying thing

where it convinces
my body it's

f
a
l
l
i
n
g

I FLINCH IN MY HAMMOCK

Startled awake.

My hammock
rocks sideways.

Now,
      I'm
      actually
      falling.

            Out
            of my
            hammock.

                  Onto
                  the floor.

I rub my hip.
It's going to bruise.

      Then,
      I notice a voice
      singing outside.

      Perfect pitch.
      Sweet as
      peppermint.
      Riding the wind
      like a
      gliding kite.

PEEKING OUT MY WINDOW

The bonfire
still burns.
Its flames
sway,
like golden
wheat fields.
They reflect
on each
treehouse's
glass walls.

A shadow
sits beside
the bonfire.

The source
of the
singing.

There's
buzzing, too.

Ernestina.

ERNESTINA'S SONG

No lyrics.
Only notes
repeating
a loop.

Over
and
over,

like
stripes
on a
zebra.

It's
easy to
memorize.

Soft
as a
whisper,

I sing
along.

NIGHTLY RAIN SHOWER

Minutes later,
the weather towers
on the island hum.
Their foggy, green lights
blink at the same time.

The weather towers
puff out chubby clouds.

White, gray, and dark blue.

The clouds spread
across the sky,
hiding every
star from sight.

Violet lightning.
Rolling thunder.

Rain falls from
the human-made storm,
the way it does every night.
Giving drink to the plants.
Washing
yesterday
into the past.

I look back
at the bonfire.

Ernestina is gone.

MORNING CHORES

Harvesting
strawberries.
Filling barrels.

I hum

last night's song

as I
move
along.

LUNCHTIME

"We don't
have to skip
the whole
afternoon,"
I tell Nano.
"Let's skip for
only one hour."

"One hour
isn't too long,"
Nano shrugs.

Lupita stuffs
her yellow apple
into Nano's
mouth.

"Today's afternoon chores
are at the spider farm,"
Lupita huffs at Nano.
"I won't let you
skip that!"

THE SPIDER FARM

houses hundreds
of species of spiders.
We collect their webs.
Turn web
into thread.

Nano's moms
are spider farmers.
That's why he's
been obsessed with
bugs since we were
young as larvae.

Nano's dream is
to engineer the
next generation
of fashion on

Isla Sola.

Not only to
look cooler,
but to
keep us cooler
beneath the
blistering sun.
In a way that
uses less energy
than our current
clothing does.

I DON'T HAVE DREAMS LIKE NANO

Dreams to make

Isla Sola

an even more
efficient place.

Make our home
greener. Cleaner.
Do more while
wasting less.

Everyone else has
a dream like that.

Lupita's dad, Rodolfo,
wants to turn our
coral necklaces into
solar-powered batteries.

I've never
had the drive to
do more for my community.

Maybe because
I don't feel a part
of the community
the way everyone
else seems to.

LUPITA REFUSES

to let
Nano skip
the next day, too.

Even though
the day's afternoon chore
is scraping bird poop
off the solar panels.

Neither of them laughs
when I joke that someone
should invent birds
that don't poop.

When nobody
is watching,

I sneak away.

Snag my surfboard
out from my parents' closet

where they tried hiding it.

Then, head for

the beach.

CALLING THESE WAVES BIG

doesn't do
them justice.

They're taller
than palm trees.

Louder
than
thunder.

It's not a rule
to stay out of
the ocean
when waves
are this wild.

It's more
common sense.

Knowing
I shouldn't
do something
makes me
want to
do it
more.

JUMPING IN WAS A BAD DECISION

Within seconds,
I'm fighting for
my life.

I hug my
surfboard to
stay afloat.
To keep
from

sinking.

Gagging.

    Wheezing.

        I gasp for air.

            Spit out salt water.

                Blow out *mocos*.

A WAVE CRASHES OVER ME

Foamy bubbles.
Aqua water.
Gritty sand.

It pushes
me down.

Beneath
the waves.

My arms
stroke.

I need air . . .

My legs
kick.

I need air . . .

I wriggle
toward
the light.

I need air . . .

I REALLY NEED AIR!

My neck
      tightens
like a knot.
      Spasms
every time
      my brain
thinks to
      breathe.
      While I
           try to swim
faster,
        waves keep
rolling in.
        Forcing me
           different
           directions
             that aren't
               up.
           One rips
into me.
           Spins me
like a windmill.

        All

          sense

      of

              direction

          is

            gone.

In.
And out.
Of being
awake.

Dark. Passed out.

 Light. Awake.

My gut
cramps.

Dark. Passed out.

 Light. Awake.

I breathe.

Water fills
my lungs.

 Dark.

 Passed out.

 Dark . . .

35

WHEN LIGHT RETURNS

it's too bright
to see.

Salt water shoots
out my mouth
like a geyser.

Clumps of sand
fill my fists.
I'm lying on
the beach.

I turn

my head.

My foggy

vision sharpens.

I'm not

alone.

A STRANGER

with ashy brown skin
and sunburnt cheeks
kneels beside me.
Dripping wet.
He looks to be my age,
but isn't dressed
anything like me.
Oversized jade pants
tucked into black boots.
A thermal that likely
used to be white,
with a raggedy vest.
Dingy. Dirty.
Like neither his
clothes nor skin
has ever touched soap.

Most unique is
his shaggy,
baby-blue hair.
I've never seen
hair that reminds
me of the sky.

"Take it slow."
His voice is deep.
"I think you died
for a few seconds."

~~~

I scrunch
my forehead.
Arch one eyebrow.

"Well, technically, I'm not
a medical professional."
His maroon lips move fast.

"Same,"
I cough.
"So what?"

"So, I can't confirm if you
did die at any point or not."

"Well, am I
dead right now?"

"I repeat: I am *not*
a medical professional."
He takes my hands and
sits me up.
"But I'm pretty sure
you're alive right now."

"Thanks, doc."

"It's Mateo."

"Mateo,"
I correct myself.
"I'm Veny."

I steady
my breaths.

Fully realize
what's happening.

I'm sitting with
someone who
is not from
my community.

    No such thing
    has ever been
    heard of.

    We've always
    been taught that

    nothing
    exists
    beyond
    the ocean.

        No humans
        exist
        off
        of

        Isla Sola.

I SCOOT BACK

"Don't worry,"
Mateo says.
"I'm confused, too."

I say,
"Where are
you from?"

"I was about to ask
you the same thing."

I stay quiet.

"Can you at least
tell me where we are?"

Our deep
brown eyes
stare into
one another's.
Like they
might uncover
a secret if they
look hard enough.

I can't
tell if
his bones
can be
trusted.

"Are you normally
this thankful
toward others who
save your life?"

"For someone
who isn't a
medical professional,
you're good at
sarcasm."

"Are doctors sarcastic
where you're from?"

"No,"
I say
matter-of-factly.

"Then . . ."

I hate when
my back talk
comes out senseless.

"Then . . ."

"Then, can you
finally tell me
where we are?"

I say,
"Thought you
wanted to know
where I'm from?"

    Mateo says,
    "You're being
    annoying."

"What're you
doing here?"

    "Bruh!
    One question at a time.
    You're going to overload
    my brain's circuits."

I stay quiet.

    He points at the ocean.
    "I'm from out there!
    Happy?!
    Now, tell me
    where we are."

"Thought you
wanted to know
where I'm from?"

MATEO THROWS HIS ARMS UP

He jumps
to his feet.
Kicks sand.

Mateo yells,
"Your mouth
was better off
filled with salt water!"

I stand up.
"Doesn't take much
to fire you up, huh?"

He stomps
up to me.
My chest inflates
like a puffer fish.
Our noses
are a hair
apart.

"I'm more flammable
than you know, Veny."

"That why you got
all that sunburn?"

Mateo says,
"All that what?"

"Sunburn!"
I tap his
scorched
cheeks.

He shields his
face with one hand.
"Ouch!"
His other hand
pushes me away.
"Jerk!"

I giggle,
like it's
a game.

Maybe it is.

Both our heads
swiftly turn when
we hear
my name
shouted
in the

distance.

MATEO DUCKS

behind a large
sand dune.

I do
the same.

Far off,
Lupita walks
along the beach.
She carries a piece
of my shattered
surfboard.

> "Please."
> Mateo squeezes
> my shoulder.
> "Don't tell her
> about me."

I shrug
him away.
"Why are you
hiding from her?"

> "From anyone!"

"Why?"

> "Stop asking
> me questions!"

OF COURSE

I ask Mateo
another question,
"You don't
enjoy questions?"

    Mateo hisses,
    "I saved your life!"

"Didn't ask
you to."

    "Please. If you do
    nothing else for me,
    do this.
    Don't tell her or
    anyone about me."

We're back to
looking each other
dead in the eye,
like it's
instinct.

Lupita keeps
shouting,
"Veny!"

    Mateo's bottom lip
    quivers when he
    whispers,
    "Please, Veny."

I POINT MY CHIN

at the nearby
forest's edge.

I say,
"When she
looks away,
get in there.
Fast as you can."

Mateo says,
"What about you?"

"What about me?"

He rolls his eyes.

"Will you come
find me after?"

"Whatever you do,
don't eat the pink berries,"
I tell him.
"You'll lose
ten pounds.
It's not pretty.
Rivers are good for
drinking, though."

RUNNING OUT FROM BEHIND THE DUNE

"Hey! Over here!"
I wave my hands
over my head.

　　　"Veny!"
　　　Lupita responds.

I run up
to her
to keep
her away
from Mateo.

"Waves are kinda
intense today."
I stick my
tongue out.

　　　"I thought
　　　you were dead!"
　　　Lupita smacks me
　　　with my broken
　　　surfboard.

"Figured you'd
choose waves
over chores,"
I smirk.
"Where's your
boy toy?"

My arm wraps
around the back
of her neck.
I gently pull
her along
with me.
Our backs
face Mateo.

Lupita says
something.
I don't
hear it.
Because as
she speaks,
I look over
my shoulder.
Watch Mateo's blue
bird's nest disappear
into the forest.

"Did you hear me, Veny?!"
Lupita pushes me.
"It's Nano's *abuela*.
She's passing on."

PASSING ON

Our community
assembles in
Passing Meadows.
It's a clearing outside
the northern end
of our village.

We sit in the
soft green grass,
around a mound
covered in wildflowers.
Like a rainbow draped
across the earth.
Monarchs flutter
over the mound,
weaving between
Nano and his family.
They stand around
Elder Lydia,
who lies at the top
of the mound.

Whenever
someone dies,
this is how
we see them off.

Elder Lydia is passing on
from this life to the next.
Where her body will return
to the water, air, and earth.

Next to
Elder Lydia
lies her staff.
Each member of

The Council

has one.

Winding
driftwood.
Patches of
green moss.
A pink conch
fastened
at the top.

ELDER LYDIA

becomes so still,
the monarchs
begin to rest on
her body.

Hundreds.

Until she's
fully hidden
beneath their
powdery
wings.

Stillness.

Silence.

She has passed.

Shofars blow.
Their wails
climb high,
like kids
up trees.

    Echoing

    above us,

    above the
    sky's blue,

    all the way
    to the sun.

This causes
the monarchs
to scatter.

Reaching places
Lydia's energy
now occupies.

    Everywhere.

LUPITA'S FATHER, RODOLFO

is first to stand
when silence follows.

His beaded gold jewelry glows.
They're samples of new tech
he's inventing to
power machines
with solar energy.

Rodolfo was
Elder Lydia's
apprentice.

He takes her staff,
blows the conch.

The other
members of

The Council

blow their conches
in response.

Rodolfo now
serves as a
member of

The Council.

THAT NIGHT

After dinner,
there's no
song and dance.

Each person
prepares a gift
to offer
Nano's family.

Something
personal,
to share in
their loss.

Mom prepares
cuttings from her
golden pothos vines.

Dad prepares a
bundle of the sage
he grows for
Mom's hair.

I prepare to
sneak away.

SEARCHING FOR MATEO IN THE FOREST

My tiny
flashlight
guides
the way.

I shout,
"Mateo!"

Macaws in
the trees are
startled into
the air,
like
bursting
dandelions.

> Then,
> something
> large
> rustles the
> branches
> above me.

MATEO COMES CRASHING DOWN

No biggie
for him.

I break

his

fall!

We both
end up
on the
ground.

I push him off.
"What you doing
up there?!"

    "Hiding."
  He rolls over.

"What does
hiding mean
where *you*
come from?"

"Already with
the questions,"
Mateo groans.
"And attitude."

I click my tongue,
"What attitude?"

"What attitude?"
Mateo mocks.

I pull out a small
baggie from
my vest pocket.

"Guess you're
not hungry then."

I wave it
in his face.

He rolls his eyes.

I wave
it more.

"Give me that."
He swipes it fast.

"For the record,
I let you take it."

MATEO SNIFFS THE BAGGIE

He empties its
mango crisps
into his palm.

Mateo looks at me
with a stank face.
"Um . . ."

I make his
same face,
with twice
the stank.
"Um . . .
You're welcome!"

"What is it?"

"Now it's you
with the questions?"

He sniffs the food.

"For real?
I've broken
five rules
to bring you
this food."

Mateo says,
"Food's different
where I'm from."

"And I'm still
waiting to know
where that is."
I point my flashlight
at his face.

Mateo squints.
Takes a bite into
the pile in his hand.
Like he really hasn't
eaten this before.

He chews with
an open mouth,
like a baby sloth.

"They don't teach
you manners where
you're from?"

He ignores me.

Takes another bite.

MATEO TOSSES THE BAGGIE

over his shoulder.
It lands on the
forest floor,
like a fallen leaf.

"That's worse than
having no manners."
I crawl over to the
baggie and snatch
it off the ground.
"That's wasteful!"

Mateo talks
while chewing.
"You going to use
that same dirty bag
every time you bring
me food?"

I blow dirt
off the baggie.

"Good as new."

I stuff it back
in my pocket.

DOWN TO BUSINESS

We stay seated
on the ground,
not far apart.

"Look,"
I say.
"I need to
know where
you're from."

Mateo takes
his last bite.
"Why do you want
to know so badly?"

"Because this
is unheard of!
Someone existing
off Isla Sola
changes history!"

"Interesting name
for this place,"
Mateo smirks.
"Isla Sola."

I CHUCK A ROCK AT MATEO

He laughs as
it bounces off
his chest.

I scrunch
my forehead.
"You're
manipulative!"

"Am not."
Mateo licks crumbs
off his palm.
"You're overly
emotional."

"There's nothing
wrong with being
emotional!"

"I didn't say
emotional.
I said *overly*
emotional.
Big difference.
Emotions
are natural.
But you let them
control you to
the point that they
make you say and do
stuff you later regret."

63

~~~

"Anyways,"
I groan loudly.
"Where you from?"

Mateo says,
"Do your people
really not know
about the rest of
the world?"

I say,
"It's nothing
but ocean.
That's why
we stay here."

Mateo leans back.
Looks away.

"What're
you not
saying?"

"Y'all have never
left Isla Sola? Ever?"

BEYOND THE OCEAN

I say,
"No. We've always
been told there are
no other lands.
No other humans.
Which is why meeting
you is a huge shock!"

    "Humans,"
    Mateo clears
    his throat.
    Pauses.
    "Humans exist
    far and wide
    across the planet.
    Most live underground.
    The rest of the planet
    looks . . . different . . .
    from here."

"How can
that be?!"

    "You're better off
    not knowing more."

"I need
to know
everything!"

MATEO STARES ME DOWN

As if it's
his turn to
wonder if
my bones
can be trusted.

> "You have a
> happy little life
> on this happy
> little island,"
> Mateo says.
> "You don't need
> to worry what the
> rest of the world
> is up to."

"Pfft,"
I throw him
the middle finger.
"Who says I'm
happy here?"

> "Enough with the
> whole punk act,"
> Mateo whines.
> "You're not
> fooling me!
> You're only
> a big brat!"

~~~

I yell,
"You don't know
anything about me!"

>"I know you
>try to act tough,"
>Mateo yells over me.
>"But what this little
>island considers tough
>is considered squishy
>anywhere else."

My fists
clench closed like
oysters.

>"Consider yourself
>lucky
>for not knowing
>how tough the rest
>of this world is."

>Mateo sighs loudly.
>Lays himself flat.

>"Honestly, I'm jealous
>of you for not knowing."

I say,
"That doesn't mean
my life here is perfect."

> "Didn't say it was,"
> Mateo folds his hands
> behind his head.
> "No worthwhile life
> is lived in perfect comfort.
> But you have spare food
> for strangers. Rivers
> clean enough to drink freely."

"Sounds
standard
to me."

> Mateo stays quiet.

"The bare
minimum,
in fact!"

> Mateo stays quiet.

"You don't have
that back home?"

> "For someone who
> knows everything,
> you ask lots of questions."

I WANT TO KICK MATEO WHERE IT HURTS

But I'm trying
to prove him
wrong about
calling me
overly emotional.

I say,
"I'm curious about
where you're from.
I want to know more."

 "It's . . ."
 Mateo pauses.
 "It's not something
 I want to think about
 right now."

"Are you
trying to
go back?"

 "No."

"Why?"

 "For all the work it took
 to leave, talking about it
 is the last thing I want to do."

WE'RE LYING DOWN

Face up
to the
forest
canopy.

I say
nothing.

Mateo says
nothing.

It's best
to save
battery life.

I flip the
flashlight

off.

THROUGH GAPS IN THE FOREST CANOPY

Teaspoons of
starlight twinkle
across
the nighttime sky.

Owls hoot.
Crickets chirp.
Wind rocks the trees,
rustling their leaves
like wind chimes.

It carries Mateo's
scent to me.

Something
about his
sweat
stirs me.

The way
jalapeños burn
and satisfy
in the same bite.

Despite our
questions for
each other,
our mouths
stay shut.

Five minutes.

Twenty minutes.

An hour flies by.

I

doze

off

a

few

times.

I SIT UP AND STRETCH

I say,
"I should
head back.
My parents
are likely
trying to
find me."

"A rebellious son,"
Mateo huffs.
"Maybe you're a
little punk after all."

"You'll be fine
out here alone?"

Mateo's left
dimple caves.

"Back to being squishy."

I shine the
flashlight
in his eyes.

Mateo shields his
face and giggles.
"I wouldn't be mad
if you brought more
food tomorrow night."

I say,
"You expect
this to be a
nightly event?"

Mateo says,
"Easier to
keep your

secrets

in the
dark."

BACK AT HOME

My parents
ask where
I've been.

I tell them,
"Nano really
loved his
abuela.
I couldn't
leave him
to mourn
alone."

Mom straightens
the dodo feathers
in my mohawk.
"He's lucky to
have a friend
as thoughtful
as you."

Dad pats
my back.
"Being thoughtful
of others keeps
our community
healthy."

IN MY COZY HAMMOCK

Beneath
a thick,
toasty
blanket,

in my
family's
safe
home,

I have a
harder
time
relaxing
than I
did out
in the
forest
with

a stranger.

I SKIP SKIPPING CHORES

If I do
what I'm
supposed
to do, then
nobody will
pay attention
to me

That'll
make it
easier
for me
to sneak

away

at night.

With
every
churn
of the
compost
pile,

I wonder
what Mateo
is doing.

LUNCH HOUR

Nano and Lupita
are nowhere
to be found.

I eat
alone.

      Nobody
      is looking.

      A handful
      of

      protein-
      powdered
      rose petals

      slips into
      my pocket.

DINNER

Nano and Lupita
are still nowhere
to be found.

I eat
alone.

Again.

Nobody
is looking.

Four strips
of

grilled
nopales

slip into
my pocket.

NIGHTLY STORYTIME

I snake through
the mass of
teens headed
for storytime with
Elder Ernestina.

I bump into Lupita.
Nano isn't with her.

"Where y'all been?"
I ask her.

She rolls her eyes.
Brushes past me.

I don't get why.

When I move past
the last of the herd,
a bony hand
hooks my shoulder.

Bees buzz
around me.

"Wrong direction, *mijito*,"
a familiar voice says.

ERNESTINA'S PECAN EYES

stare into mine.

They're clear
as crystal.
Nothing can
get past them.

That doesn't mean
I won't try.

I say,
"I'm looking
for Nano."

"Such a thoughtful friend."
Ernestina pats my back.
Turns me to walk
the same direction
as everyone else.
"He always speaks
so warmly of you."

"Then you
understand
how important
it is for me to
find him.
With the loss of
Elder Lydia
still fresh in
his thoughts."

81

Ernestina says,
"Nano knows
as well as you do,
as well as I do,
that death is a door.
One of many doors
to many rooms
on this planet
housing us.
In this room,
she was Lydia,
from child to elder.
In the next room,
she may be water
encasing coral reefs.
Or wind
spreading willow seeds.
Or sunlight
waking sleepers at dawn.
Regardless
of the room,
she remains
a piece of
our home;
this planet.
A piece of
all of us.
Thus,
she never
leaves us."

~~~~

I slowly say,
"This great,
big planet?"

She says,
"Our beautiful
island, yes!
The whole of
our world."

Isabella
joins us.

Hurries
us both

to the
bonfire.

ERNESTINA HUMS

a childhood
song.

Everyone
can
sing
it by
heart.

Ernestina
hasn't
sung it
to us for

years.

We strum
our fingernails

to keep

the beat.

LITTLE CAPYBARA

Ernestina sings,

"Little Capybara,
youngest of his kind.

Was only a pup,
but mama knew he'd grow up,
to be the greatest of his time.

Little Capybara,
smartest of his kind.

Was only a pup,
but solved the riddles cooked up
by the elders of his tribe.

Little Capybara,
lost his way one day.

Was only a pup,
but chose to give up
on the low and humble life."

Ernestina says,

"Because
Little Capybara
was so smart,
he easily became bored
with simple chores.
The kind that little ones
are responsible for.

Cleaning.
Cooking.
Collecting.

Simple chores.
The kind that
teach little ones
important values.

Little Capybara
thought he was
too smart for them.

He thought he was

above it all."

Ernestina says,
"Little Capybara
dreamed of becoming
friends with the stars.
High up in the sky.
Away from the forest floor,
where capybaras belong.
Little Capybara went to
Kapok Tree, old and wise.
Whose branches knew
each star by name.
Little Capybara asked
to climb up
Kapok Tree, so he,
too, could know
each star by name.
Kapok Tree told
Little Capybara,
You must stay safe
on the forest floor
where capybaras belong!

Little Capybara
wouldn't listen.

Little Capybara
thought he was
smarter than
sound reason."

Ernestina flows
between
speaking and singing,

"Little Capybara
started to climb up
Kapok Tree.
Up! Up! Up he went!"

But Little Capybara's
hands and feet
were meant for
the forest floor.
Not for climbing trees.

It wasn't long before
Little Capybara slipped
off Kapok Tree's branches.

Little Capybara
had a great fall!
Tumbling! Tumbling!

All the way down!
Until he cracked his head
like an egg on the ground!

So, what do we learn from
Little Capybara's song?"

WE RECITE THE LAST LYRIC

back to Ernestina,

"To listen

to reason.

To stay safe

where

we belong."

AFTERWARD

The teens

disperse.

I think to
ask Lupita
what she's
so angry
about.

Instead,

I

vanish

into

the

night.

TREKKING THROUGH THE FOREST

I softly whistle
Ernestina's song
from the other night.

It's been stuck
in my head,

like sand in shorts
after surfing.

"Catchy tune!"
Mateo's voice
makes me jump.

His head
pops out
from a pile
of brush.

"This hideout
works better
than I planned!"

I say,
"Better than you
falling on me, again."
I walk over.
"Wait. How'd
you build that?"

MATEO'S HIDEOUT

He covered a hard,
dome structure
with brush
and mud.

I knock on the dome,
"What is this?"

      "You live on an island,"
      Mateo says.
      "You've never seen a boat?"

"Now you're
question-happy?"

      "It's called a boat.
      They're for traveling
      over water. This is what
      brought me here."

"What's it
made from?"

      "Plastic."

"Weird."

      "You're weird."

A SPARK OF NEON BLUE LIGHT

buzzes over
my shoulder.
It flies into
Mateo's face.

Mateo jumps back,
Swats the air.
It quickly turns
from blue to red.

"Don't hurt it!"
I grab Mateo's hands.
Hold them in place.

    "What is it?"

"A flicker fly.
It's harmless."

    "Red is the least
    harmless color!"

"It's red
because
of you."

MY POINTER FINGER

sticks out
like a perch.

"They're sensitive
little critters,"
I say.
"Their colors reflect
your mood based off
what they smell in
your sweat."

We watch the
floating red light
bob through the air.
Until it rests
on my
pointer finger.

It turns from red,
to blue,
to purple.

Mateo says,
"What does
purple feel like?"

"A mix of
blue and red."

~~~

Mateo says,
"Red is our
common ground."

I say,
"Unsure what
red means to you."

"I'd say anger."

"Probably so."

"I don't see why.
You have it made.
Home. Friends.
Shelter. Food."

"Blue for me
means lonely.
And the lonely
causes anger."

"Seems my loneliness
has lasted so long that
now it's fully anger."

"You don't
seem angry."

"Some of us are
better programmed
to hide our emotions."

"Wish I was."

"No. You don't."

The flicker fly
crawls over my
fingertips.

With my free hand,
I take Mateo's hand.

He tries to pull
away at first.

Then
gives way.

I pull his hand to
my hand holding
the flicker fly.

PRISM

Our hands gently press
flat against each other.

Palm to palm.

Swirling fingerprints
to swirling fingerprints.

The flicker fly crawls
over my thumb.
Onto Mateo's thumb.
It's six tiny legs
trail back and forth
from Mateo's hand to mine.

The flicker fly
changes colors.

From purple,

to red. Like angry.
To orange. Like brave.
To yellow. Like curious.
To green. Like envious.
To blue. Like lonely.

Back to
purple.

Like a mix of
me and Mateo.

THE FLICKER FLY FLASHES WHITE

Like a
strobe
light.

A twig snaps
within the
dark brush.

We jolt our hands
back to our sides.

The flicker fly is
flung into the brush.

Mateo and I
face the direction
of the snapped twig.

My

      flashlight

          beams

             ahead.

NANO AND LUPITA ARE WATCHING US

Lupita gasps,
"What the—"

I rush up to
them and say,
"Don't freak out!"

Nano's
jaw
drops
open,

like a
catfish.

Lupita points her
flashlight at Mateo
"Who the—"

I say,
"Let me
explain!"

AFTER EXPLAINING

Lupita nods at
Mateo's hair.
"He part
peacock?"

Mateo says,
"Blue hair
is common
where I'm from."

Lupita says,
"Which is where?"

I say,
"Still waiting
for him to say."

Lupita stomps
up to Mateo.
"I can get it
out of him."

Nano
speaks up,
"No, Lupita!"

~~~~~

Nano says,
"The Council
can deal with him."

I say,
"They can't
know about him."

Nano says,
"They have to!
You can't keep
this a secret!"

Lupita says,
"I'm shocked
they haven't
found out yet."

I say,
"They've
been busy
with . . ."
I look at Nano.
Then at Lupita.
"With your dad
joining The Council."

Nano's
shoulders

drop.

Mateo says,
"They can't know about me!"

Lupita walks up to
Mateo's makeshift hideout,
"You gonna hide in this
wannabe turtle shell forever?"

Mateo says,
"It's actually super durable."

Lupita reaches out her foot and
lightly nudges Mateo's hideout.

It topples over.

Mateo groans,
"Rude!"

Lupita says,
"Only trying to prove a point.
You won't last on your own.
You need to join our community."

I help Mateo flip the boat
back upside down.

Lupita says,
"Aside from your needs,
our community needs to know
humans exist off of Isla Sola."

MATEO MARCHES UP TO LUPITA

"How do you know
they don't already know?"

Nano forces himself
between them.
"Impossible! Our community
values the exchange of information.
That's how we evolve as humans."

Nano's bull-like nostrils flair.
His chubby cheeks burn rosy.

I place my hands on
Nano's and Mateo's chests.
Gently push them apart.

I say,
"Chill, Nano.
He didn't mean it
any type of way."

I come
face-to-face
with Nano.

He won't look
me in the eye.

I WAIT FOR NANO

to say
something.

He breathes
heavy.

"Nano,"
I say,
"What's going on?
It isn't like you
to get riled up."

"*Pos*,"
Nano's voice is shaky.
"It's not like
my *abuela* died
and my best friend
hasn't checked on me
even once.
Or like he's out here
keeping secrets
from me."

I say,
"Nano, I couldn't—"

～～～

Nano cuts me off,
"I know you lied about
going to check on me, Veny.
Your mom asked me to
make sure you weren't
overstaying your welcome,
being late at my house these
past nights to keep me company.
Because I'm mourning.
Because my freaking *abuela* died.
And I'll never hear her call me
lindo again. Or anything else.
Ever again.

Don't worry, Veny.
I lied for you. Like always.
I played along. Said you weren't
overstaying your welcome.
You were being a good friend.
A brother. Even though you haven't
said one word to me this whole time!"

Nano whimpers.

I wrap him
in a hug.

His arms stay
at his sides.

I hug him tighter.
"I'm sorry."

~~~~

Nano's hot tears
burn my collarbone.

A cold, heavy weight
settles over my chest.

The kind of guilt
that never fully lifts.

I say,
"I've been a
bad friend.
I'm sorry."

My eyes water from
the ache passed into me
each time Nano shakes
from sobbing.

I feel extra lonely,
even with my body
against my best friend.

We cry together
in front of the
last two people
either of us
wants to show
our squishiest
side to.

NANO STEADIES HIS BREATH

His temple
rests against
my temple.

He hugs
me back.

I apologize

more.

He tells me
it's okay.

That

he

understands.

My guilt
makes me
feel tiny.

I PLUCK OUT SEVERAL

dodo feathers
from my hair.

Nano's head is
shaved clean,
except for a
single braid
on the back
of his head.

It runs
down
to his
waist.

I stick my
dodo feathers
into Nano's braid.

I say,
"Brother."

Rest my
forehead
against
Nano's.

      Nano replies,
      "Brother."

AFTER GIVING US A MOMENT

Lupita breaks the silence.
"We followed you
out here because
we had to know
what you were
actually up to."

I say,
"Now you know
everything."

Lupita looks at Mateo.
"Not quite everything."

NEXT DAY'S CHORES

Harvest honey.

Rake leaves.

Wash linens.

Nonstop
chores
make
the day
fly by.

For dinner,
hibiscus tacos.

Juicy
and
sweet.

Grapes
for
dessert.

I pocket
what
I can.

110

MATEO LOVES THE HIBISCUS TACOS

He
inhales
them,

like a
blue heron
gulping
rainbow trout.

Between me,
Nano, and Lupita,
we brought
Mateo

four.

111

MATEO ASKS ABOUT

our island.

We give
him an
earful.

From
mesquite trees
        to mushrooms.

Tapirs
        to toucans.

Inchworms
        to iguanas.

Weather towers.
Greenhouses.
Solar panels.

Mateo
acts like

Isla Sola

is an
alien
planet.

IT'S MATEO'S TURN

to talk about
his home.

He still won't
say much.

"It's

nothing

like here,"
is all Mateo says.

 Afterward,
 Nano
 and
 Lupita
 cuddle up.

 Whispers
 between
 minutes
 of sloppy
 making out.

  Mateo
  and I
  talk to
  drown
  out their
  smacks.

ME AND MATEO

I say,
"If you won't
talk about where
you're from,
then tell me
about you."

      Mateo says,
      "Do you really
      care to know?"

"Nope,"
I smirk.
"Tell me
anyway."

      "I don't know
      what to say.
      I've never
      talked about
      myself before."

"Favorite color?"

      "Maroon."

"Boring!"

MAROON

Mateo says,
"It's not boring!"

I say,
"Convince me."

"Maroon is present,
but also hidden.
It's not quite red.
Not quite brown.
It takes up space
between two worlds.
Calls both worlds home,
while creating a
place to claim as its own."

"Figured blue
would be your
favorite."
I tug his hair.

He laughs.
Swats me away.
"Seriously?
Because of
my hair?"

NOT JUST ANY BLUE

I say,
"Blue's not a
bad choice."

      Mateo asks,
      "Oh, really?"

"Yes, *really*.
It's my favorite."

      "Any blue?"

"Not just
any blue.
The sky's blue
during the middle
of the day. Noon.
When there are no
shadows trailing
ahead or behind.
The sun is exactly
above us. And it
makes the sky look
endless. Far off.
Yet within reach.
Like distance is
only an illusion.
The purest blue
Mother Nature
can gift us."

116

MOTHER NATURE

Mateo says,
"I still don't get the
Mother Nature deal.
Y'all always mention it."

I say,
"My community
trusts in science.
That's how we
make sense of
the world around us.
How all its pieces fit.
And the glue
holding it
together—
the why behind it all?
We believe that's
something special.
Something we
can't totally grasp.
But it's also something
we carry.
Through us. In us.
In every natural being.
The energy of
all living things.
It binds us together.
Makes us want to
protect life in all forms.
We call it
Mother Nature."

Mateo says,
"I still don't get it."

I say,
"It's not really
something
to get."

Mateo's eyes
yearn to see
what I see.

"So, when the sky
is my favorite blue,
I know the science behind
why it's that shade of blue.
But that part of me that
is in awe of it still?
The part of me that wants
to protect the sky so it can
always turn that shade of blue?
That's Mother Nature in me."

"Maybe I wasn't
programmed with
Mother Nature in mind."

"You were.
Unless you're
not human,"
I snicker.

Mateo frowns.
Folds his arms.
Shrinks his neck
and shoulders inward.

"I'm joking,"
I reach out
and squeeze
his surprisingly
firm bicep.
"You were raised
to see life differently
than me.
You'll catch on
in time."

Mateo's muscles
loosen in my grip.
He nods. Smiles.

I pull my
hand back.
Readjust my
white coral
necklace.

"Does everyone
in your community
wear one of those?"

MATEO EASILY UNDERSTANDS

when I explain
the purpose of
white coral necklaces.

     Mateo asks,
     "Your village is
     so calculated.
     How is it you'd
     be the odd-numbered
     kid left unpaired?"

I say,
"I wasn't planned.
They didn't think
my mom could get
pregnant. Until she did."

     "Stubborn
     since the
     womb."

We laugh.

"Did you have
anyone like that
back home?"

"Like that?"
Mateo points his
chin at Nano and Lupita.
They somehow haven't
turned blue from the lack
of air while making out.

"Maybe not that
insanely horny,"
I laugh.
"But yeah.
A girlfriend."

"Not at all.
There were girls, yeah.
But I never felt anything
for any of them."

"What about boys?"

"I definitely felt things
for boys back home.
But, nah,
I would have never
given any of them a
coral necklace."

Mateo pauses.

"What about you?
Which do you feel
things for?"

～～～

I say,
"I like
all genders.
Even still,
I'm single
for life."

　　Mateo says,
　　"Maybe Mother Nature
　　hasn't glued you to
　　the right piece yet."

"That's not . . ."

That's
not the
correct
way to
reference
Mother Nature.

"You know what?
Maybe you're right."

WE TALK MORE

About
everything.

About
nothing.

Our voices
fall softer
with every
sentence.

Until our
whispers
are mumbles.

Until our
mumbles
are breaths.

Until
sleep
claims
us both.

THUNDER WAKES US

It's drizzling.

Nano panics.
"We're dead
for being out
this late!"

I say,
"We'll come up
with an excuse."

Drizzle
turns
to rain.

Lupita says,
"We're about
to get soaked."

Mateo waves,
"Follow me!
I know where
we can stay dry."

~~~~

Lupita says,
"No! We're going
back home!"

Nano says,
"Lupita's right.
Let's go, Veny!"

They run off,
expecting me
to follow.

I tell Mateo,
"I'll wait out
the storm
with you."

He nods.
Runs the
opposite
direction
of them.

I follow.

WE BLITZ

through
mud, brush,
and rainstorm.

We enter a region
where the ground
is rocky. Boulders
and rain puddles
form a maze.

Lightning and
thunder grow,
as if they're
fed by my fear.

Mateo reaches back.
Grabs my trembling hand.

We reach a rock wall
with a cave entrance.

Mateo drags me in.

I reach for my
flashlight.
Light up our view.

My gut

sinks.

INSIDE THE CAVE

Long stalactites
hang high above.
Stalagmites grow
alongside the jagged
tunnel walls.

I gasp,
"We shouldn't
be here, Mateo."

Mateo smirks,
"Not so punk now, huh?"

"How'd you
even know
about it?"

"I followed
adults from
your village."

"Crud."

I say,
"Those adults are
The Council.
Only they're
allowed in here."

Mateo says,
"Why?"

"This is where
they meet."

"Why so secretive?"

"Just is."

"Your community
values the exchange
of information.
Why would they
exchange information
in secret?"

"Mateo. We can get
in serious trouble
for being here."

"Who'll snitch?"

I say,
"Let's go."

Mateo says,
"Let's at least
wait out the storm.
Together."

"If they
find us here—"

"Who, Veny?
You think anyone will
be out in this weather?"

Mateo turns away.

"Let's look around."
Mateo marches deeper.

Into
gross
darkness.

"Wait!"

I shine my
flashlight.

MATEO WHISTLES ERNESTINA'S SONG

The notes bounce
off the tunnel walls.

I say,
"How do you
know that song?"

    Mateo says,
    "You whistled it
    last night.
    While you were
    looking for me."

"How long were you
listening to me whistle?"

    "Roughly
    twenty-one seconds."

"You
memorized
it that fast?"

    "Yes."

"Guess you'd say,
*I was programmed
to memorize quickly.*"

~~~

Mateo says,
"Correct."

Before I can
sass him,
we reach the
tunnel's end.

We enter a huge,
warm cavern.

Purple crystals
cover the walls
and ceiling,
as if we're
inside a geode.

The crystals shimmer,
like moonlight reflected
off ocean surface.
Illuminated by
a firepit
in a brass bowl
at the center
of the cavern.

Circling the bowl
are 15 stools.
One for each
member of

The Council.

|3|

THE COUNCIL'S CAVERN

Mateo rushes ahead
and looks closely
at the purple crystals.

     Mateo says,
     "What is this?"

I say,
"Amethyst."

     "Nah. Too dense."

"You can tell
its density by
looking at it?

Mateo ignores me.

He grazes his
pointer finger
over the crystal wall.

     "Ow!"

He jolts his hand
away. Sucks on his
pricked finger before
blood drips

out.

I WANT TO MAKE FUN OF MATEO

for cutting himself.

But I stay

quiet

in hopes

he'll get

bored.

Decide to

leave.

Without

him realizing

I've

tricked him

into it.

133

TO ANNOY HIM

I softly hum

Ernestina's song.

Mateo doesn't react.

I hum louder.
Enough to echo
through
the cavern.

One of the
purple crystals
starts to
glow.

MATEO RUNS

to the glowing crystal.

I shout,
"Be careful!"

The crystal
stops glowing.

      Mateo says,
      "How'd that happen?"

"No clue.
But let's take
it as a sign.
Time to leave."

      "That song!"

"Huh?"

      "That song you
      were humming."

"But how—"

Mateo hums
the song.
Off-key.

Nothing
happens.

〜〜〜

     Mateo says,
     "Sing it!"

I say,
"Mateo."

     "Sing it!
     Then, we'll go.
     Promise!"

I exhale
loudly,
"Alright!"

I join
Mateo.

Sing

from
my belly.

Each note in,

     if I do
     say so
     myself,

perfect pitch.

THE CRYSTAL GLOWS

brighter
than
before.

Mateo grabs my hand.
"Don't stop! Keep singing!"

The crystal rings
like a bell.

It shines a
purple laser

into the
firepit.

In the flames,
purple lines appear.

They worm.

Bend.

Shape into footage.

People. My community.
Dancing. Rejoicing.
Me. Nano. Lupita.
All the other teens.
Sitting beside the bonfire.
Ernestina telling stories.

THIS FOOTAGE

It's from the night
I was woken by

Ernestina

singing this song.

Out of the
corner of my eye,
Mateo swats the air.

A mosquito.
Probably.

I'm too
fixated
on the
footage
to care.

Ernestina
is alone
in the flames.
Seated beside the
village bonfire. Singing.
She quickly turns her head.
Looks over her shoulder.

Her fiery eyes

directed at me.

STARTLED, I GASP

My
singing
echoes.

Then,
silence.

The crystal
darkens.
Vanishing the laser.
Erasing the footage.

Mateo
swats
the air.

Harder
than before.

Buzzing.

He's
surrounded

by a
swarm

of bees.

COUNTLESS MORE BEES

Buzzing loud
as a waterfall.

I try
to help
Mateo.

There are
too many
bees.

For some
reason,
they're
only
pestering
him.

Not
once is
he stung.

Then—

      Tap!
      Tap!
      Tap!

THE BEES RETREAT

to where the

      Tap!
      Tap!
      Tap!

      comes from.

I turn

that
way.

My heart drops
into my boots.

ERNESTINA STANDS THERE

tapping her
staff against
the ground.
Commanding
the bees
to leave
the cavern.

When the
cloud of
bees clears,
my head spins.

Behind
Ernestina
is the rest of

The Council

and their
apprentices.

Lupita, too,
with Rodolfo.

She mouths, *sorry*.

They must have
used her to track
me down.

BEFORE I SPEAK

Ernestina says,
"Stay away from him!"

I say,
"Ernestina—"

Ernestina growls,
"I'm not talking
to you, Veny!"

Mateo
lifts his
hands.
"I mean no harm!"

Ernestina says,
"Are there others?"

Mateo says,
"I'm alone."

Ernestina says,
"Are you being followed?"

Mateo says,
"No."

Ernestina says,
"Veny, come here."

I say,
"Ernestina,
he's no threat."

Ernestina says,
"You have no idea
the threat
he brings to

Isla Sola."

MATEO CRIES

"I'm no threat!
I swear!"

A council member laughs,
"Swear on what?
Your circuit board brain?"

I say,
"His bones can be trusted!"

Council members
laugh. I don't get
what's so funny.

I hold Mateo's hand.

The Council

gasps and squirms,
like fish out of water.

Ernestina
is unmoved.
She looks me
in the eye.

The firepit
reflects in
her pupils,
angry as a
toppled anthill.

I STARE HER BACK DOWN

Equally angry.
Equally tired.

The rest of

The Council

babbles on,
grossed out
by the sight
of my empathy
for Mateo.

Ernestina
exhales.

Her scrunched
eyebrows relax.

Her gaze
softens.

We see in each other
the same stubbornness
it takes to survive on

Isla Sola.

ErNestINA
LIFTS HER STAFF

She says,
"Council!
I call for a vote
to be made now!"

Most of them
fall quiet.

Some argue.

   This isn't the time!

Rodolfo orders
Lupita to wait
outside.

Ernestina says,
"I call for a vote.
Whether Veny can
learn the truth or not."

Some
agree.

Most
don't.

I say,
"Truth of what?"

THE COUNCIL IGNORES ME

Ernestina
sits on one of
the stools circling
the firepit.

The other
14
do the same.

My fingers
link with Mateo's,
like shoelaces.

Ernestina says,
"I call for a vote:
To tell Veny the truth of

Isla Sola

and our history."

ERNESTINA'S DEFENSE

Ernestina says,
"It's the only way
he'll see that . . . thing . . .
for what it truly is."

I hold
Mateo's
hand
tighter.

Someone argues,
"Veny might tell others."

Another says,
"Every council member before
has known. Nobody has told."

Another says,
"If Veny does tell?"

Someone says,
"Our island's ecosystem
could be put in danger."

Ernestina says,
"Or it would stay protected.
With everyone aware of
which technologies to avoid."

They debate longer.

TIME TO VOTE

To vote yes,
staffs are raised.

To vote no,
staffs are lowered.

The vote count is

8–7.

They've voted
to tell me the

truth.

ErNestiNa WAVES HER HAND

to call me over.

I stay put.
She snarls.

She hands
Isabella
her staff.

Isabella puts
the staff's conch
to her mouth.

The other
14 on

The Council

do the same
with their
conches.

They blow.
Harmonize.
Chords I've
never heard

before.

EVERY CRYSTAL IN THE CAVERN GLOWS

Bright as
the sun.

Footage
appears
in them.

As if the
crystals
form
a giant
screen.

THE TRUTH

We're shown countless people.
Crammed into tiny homes
stacked on top of each other,
reaching higher than the clouds.

The clouds. Dark. Gray.
But not a gray I know.
Mixed with black,
like smoke. It hovers.
Frozen. Green raindrops
falling onto streets
covered in trash.
Metal machines
spewing more smoke.
Bigger metal monsters
digging into the ground.
Pulling out black tar.
Black tar spilling.
Flooding beaches.
Drenching fish and birds
and shooting stars reflected
on the ocean surface.
Billions of people with
outstretched hands.
Begging for crumbs from
families hoarding resources.
Living in gold towers. They laugh.
Spit into the beggars' palms.

~~~~

Humans create machines
identical to humans,
with unnatural hair colors.
To work harder. Faster.
So the families in gold towers
can hoard more resources.

Fires rage. Skies darken.
No trees. No sunlight.
A clouded horizon.
Desperate. Hopeless.
In every direction.

My hand
lets go of
Mateo.

I drift
closer

      to the
      wall.

        The
        sights.

          This.
          world.

            This
            nightmare.

Ernestina says,
"Before

Isla Sola,

our
ancestors
lived
on lands
beyond
the ocean.
Ruled by
selfish families.
They exploited
others
to gain
resources.
Took more
than they
needed.
Left others
lacking.
Used harsh
technology
to grow their
storehouses
at the
expense
of all
living
beings."

SOLAR PUNKS

The footage shows people.
United. Marching.
Filling streets.
Outside gold towers.
With raised fists. Chanting.
Holding signs that say,

Solar Punks.

Ernestina says,
"Our ancestors
banded together.
Against corruption,
greed, and exploitation.
They hoped to save
what was left of our planet.
They were met with
fury by those in power.
Many lives were lost.
The survivors set out
to find a new home."

The footage shows
survivors coming together.
Determined, still.
Building a boat
a thousand times bigger
than Mateo's.
Covered in

solar panels.

Their boat
travels the ocean,
beneath skies filled
with endless
black clouds.

The solar panels
are useless.

They float.

       Aimless.

           For years.

Until they finally
reach waters
untouched
by dark clouds.

Beneath sunlight,
they cheer and cry.
Thank Mother Nature
for guiding their way.

Their boat
comes alive.
Sets course for

an island

on the horizon.

THEIR SONG ENDS

The crystals darken.

My skin turns cold.
My head, heavy.

All I've known
has been a lie.

Mateo walks up to me,
eyes watery.
He reaches out.

I cross my arms.

It's hard to trust
my own bones anymore.

Ernestina tells Mateo,
"Will you tell him now?
Or should we?"

I say,
"Tell me what, Mateo?"

~~~

Mateo says,
"Veny. I'm sorry."

I say,
"What is it?"

"It's not what
they think.
I swear!"

"Mateo.
Tell me."

MATEO'S TRUTH

    Mateo says,
    "I'm not exactly human."

My mouth
drops open.
No words fall out.

Rodolfo
approaches us.

    Mateo says,
    "But you need to
    believe me, Veny.
    They're wrong about me."

Rodolfo
grabs
Mateo.

Pins Mateo's
arms behind
his back.

Mateo tries to
break free,
but Rodolfo
is twice
his size.

I say,
"What are you, Mateo?"

RODOLFO DRAGS MATEO

to the firepit.
He takes Mateo's
right wrist.
Stretches
Mateo's arm.

Rodolfo says,
"I'll show you, Veny."

He forces
Mateo's hand
into the flames.

Mateo

screams

in terrible

pain.

He begs

to be

freed.

MATEO CRIES,

"I'm only half-machine!"

A council member shouts,
"There's no such thing!"

Mateo screams in pain,
"Technology elsewhere
didn't stop advancing!
Life went on without you!"

The Council's members
shout back. Their voices
like rain hitting a tin roof.

Rodolfo gasps.
Releases Mateo.

Mateo falls to the ground
and cradles his hand.
White boils cover
his brown skin.
Instead of blood,
black tar bubbles
from his open wounds.

Mateo begs
for help.

  I'm torn
  between
  two worlds.

RODOLFO'S FACE LOSES COLOR

He panics.
Runs up to

The Council

and says,
"That's real
human skin.
And tissue.
Maybe bones!"

Mateo cries,
"I'm telling you!
I'm part-machine.
Powered by the
energy sources
that destroyed the planet.
And I am also part-human.
Alive! Same as you!"

A red light begins
to blink from
Mateo's chest.
Slowly.
It shines through
his dirty thermal.

A soft alarm beeps
with each flash.

THE COUNCIL PANICS

They say Mateo
has a weapon.

"It's worse than a weapon!"
Mateo silences them.
"The rest of the world
considers me nothing
but a machine, too.
Created to work
jobs too dangerous
for full-humans.
I worked on an oil rig,
against my will.
This light and alarm,
it's a tracker.
Activated if
I'm injured.
So they can find me.
Fix me. Send me
back to work. Fast."

I say,
"If they track you down,
will they discover

Isla Sola?"

MATEO GRITS HIS TEETH

He says,
"Because of bad
pollution, far off
signals can't travel
fast through the air."

Ernestina says,
"Are we safe?"

Mateo says,
"They can't travel fast.
But they can still travel.
It's a matter of time
before they lock in
on my location."

The Council panics.

Mateo says,
"Isla Sola is not
on any map.
They'll guess I've
washed away in the
ocean. Consider me
good as dead."

I say,
"Are you sure?"

Mateo pauses.
Says, "No."

I KNEEL
BESIDE MATEO

Look into his
brown eyes.
They remind me of
soil after fresh rain.
Hungry for seeds
to, in time,
grow a harvest.

I say,
"How do we
disable the
tracker?"

    Mateo says,
    "Without proper
    tools, I have to be
    disabled entirely."

"Meaning?"

    "I have to
    be shut down."

"How do we
bring you
back after?"

    "Veny.
    It doesn't
    work like that."

~~~

I say,
"Our engineers
have ways."

Ernestina
joins us.

I say,
"Right, Ernestina?
We can disable his
tracker without
harming him?"

She says
nothing.

I cry,
"Ernestina!"

Ernestina says,
"We must disable
his tracker at once.
Or we risk the
rest of the world
learning of our
presence."

COUNCIL MEMBERS SHOUT

"Throw him
into the fire!"

Mateo begs
for his life.

Ernestina
kneels
beside us.
Stares into
Mateo's eyes.

Squints.
As if she
sees something
the others
can't.

Something
I first saw
when the
flicker fly
shined our
two lights
as one.

Ernestina says,
"We will try
to spare him.
For now."

OUTSIDE THE OPERATING ROOM

I sit with
Ernestina.

Meanwhile,
the island's
best engineers
examine Mateo.

Ernestina
convinced

The Council

to keep
Mateo alive.

> She told them,
> "Mateo can catch us up
> on the history of Earth!"

ERNESTINA
TELLS ME

"At dawn,
The Council will take a vote:
whether or not we should
tell the community
about our true history and
the rest of the planet."

I say,
"Why now?"

"We can't easily
hide a newcomer
running around
with blue hair."

"So, you do think
they'll save him?"

"I do."

I lean my head
onto her shoulder.

"I hope so."

"Hope has a way
of solving our problems.
Even outside of our
expectations."

MY TEARS DRIP

like rainfall.
They form puddles
on Ernestina's gown.
Bees come to
taste their salt.

Ernestina
pets my hair.
Readjusts the
dodo feathers.

> She says,
> "I see myself in you, Veny.
> I was an odd-numbered
> child, also. I understand
> your loneliness.
> How it makes you want
> to rebel for any reason,
> and no reason at all."

I say,
"Around Mateo,
I felt a little less
like that."

The operating room
doors swing open.

ERNESTINA IS CALLED INSIDE

In the cold,
empty hallway,

I worry I'll never
feel the way I did
with Mateo,

again.

Ernestina
returns

with
ponds
for
eyes.

"I'm sorry, Veny."

IN THE OPERATING ROOM

Mateo lies on
a silver table.
Tubes, wires, and
black tar all over.
His burnt hand is
wrapped in gauze.
His tracker
flashes red and beeps.

> Mateo says,
> "The red brings out
> the blue in my hair."

I roll my
watery eyes,
"Ridiculous."

> "You're ridiculous."

"Is this really
how you want
me to remember you?"

> "Is this how *you*
> want to remember me?"

"That pain medication's
working wonders
for your personality."

> He smiles like a donkey.

I THINK UP SCENARIOS

Wheel
Mateo
out of
here.

Make
a break
for his
boat.

Travel
far
away.

If his
location
is ever found,

we simply
keep moving.

Live on
the run.

Annoy
each other
the way
only
besties
can.

174

I SIT

on the edge of
the operating table.

I say,
"You don't have
to do this."

      Mateo says,
      "Yes, I do.
      If I don't, your whole
      community will be in
      danger. I have to do
      what's best for the whole."

"You've been here
only a few days and you
understand that
better than me."

      "Probably because
      you're the closest
      I've ever had
      to community.
      I want what's best
      for you."

I COLLECT DODO FEATHERS

from my hair.

Fill Mateo's
hair with them.

Our eyes
water.

Mateo
smiles.

He presses
my palm
against
his chest.

His strong
heartbeat
shakes my
hand.

I'm convinced
he's alive.

The way
I'm alive.

Mother Nature
is in him, too.

WE STARE INTO EACH OTHER

Like it's what
we do best.

Words pile onto
my tongue.
My mouth fills
with a dozen
confessions.
Futures
I thought
I saw.

My mouth
opens to let
them pour out.

     At the same time,
     Mateo's does too.

We quickly
apologize for
interrupting the other.

     Mateo's tracker speeds up.
     The flashing. Beeping.

     Mateo says,
     "They're about to
     lock in on my location."

WHAT HAPPENS NEXT

Engineers and
council members
rush in.

Engineers surround Mateo.

I rip off my
coral necklace.
Hold it out
to Mateo.
It's pieces fall. Scatter.
Like rabbits to their dens.

Rodolfo grabs me.
Drags me out.
I kick. Scream.
Thrash in his arms.
A needle pricks my neck.
My veins become icy.
Dizzy. Drowsy. Sedated.

All the while,
Mateo's tracker
beeps faster. Louder.

Until all
goes . . .

dark.

THE FOLLOWING TWO WEEKS

My head hangs low
wherever I go.

I have nothing to say.

To anyone.
For anything.

Chores feel pointless.
I do them anyway.

They're not going to
get done otherwise.

If I don't
do my part,
we all suffer
the consequences.

Plus,
busyness
helps me
forget to
miss

Mateo.

STILL, I SEE

his red
in every

sunrise.

His blue
in every

midday sky.

Our purple
in every

sunset.

AFTER STORYTIME WITH ERNESTINA

she plucks me
from the crowd.

Walks me
down the
northward path.

Away from others, she says,
"By tomorrow morning,
everyone will know."

She laughs at
my dropped jaw.

"It's time they knew.
It was always thought
if nobody knew of
destructive technology,
then it could never be
reproduced."

I say,
"Wouldn't it be
better to know
history? So we
know what not
to repeat?"

Ernestina says,
        "We truly
        think alike."

I say,
"We would have
hated each other
if we were born in the same
generation."

        "Is that so?"

"I'd always
be trying to
humble you."

        "Sometimes it's best
        to let people think
        they have the answers.
        In this way, their
        rebellious nature
        works in your favor."

        Ernestina hums
        the notes of her
        bonfire song.

"Wait. The song
you're humming.
Did you mean
for me
to hear it
that night?
Because
you knew
I'd one day
sneak into
the cavern?"

Ernestina smirks.

The
trail
takes
us to

Passing Meadows.

ErNESTINA
SAYS,

"I've told Isabella
that she's to select
you as her apprentice
when I pass on."

I say,
"I'm nothing like a
council member."

"Exactly why you're
perfect for the job.
Our future needs punks
like you to revolutionize
the way we live.
With technology.
And empathy."

Ernestina stops.

"I've made
arrangements
for you
on the mound."

I pull out
my flashlight.

Ernestina slaps
my hand.

Ernestina says,
"By day, the sun
guides our way.
By night, we're not
robbed of its light."

She points
to the moon.

Our reminder,
that even
in the night,
our sun is alight.

Ernestina
nudges
me forward.

I walk
to the
mound,
bathed in
moonlight.

ON THE MOUND

lies Mateo's
still body,
surrounded
by wildflowers.
Repaired flesh,
metal, and
whatever else
he's made of.

It must have taken
the engineers the past
two weeks to piece him
back together.
Perfectly.
Exactly like
the day I met him.

Except,
no air
in his
lungs.

No pulse
in his
wrist.

I suppose
this is our
proper
goodbye.

HIS BLUE HAIR

holds my gifted
dodo feathers.

Around
his neck,
my restrung
coral necklace.

Rodolfo's gold
solar power beads
are between
each coral piece.
Rodolfo's gift to
share in my loss.

I lie
with
Mateo.

Rest my
head on
his chest.

Don't
move
once
all
night.

AT DAWN

Heavy
winds
wake me
to indigo
skies.

My
eyes
look
east,
waiting
for
sunrise.

My
head
stays
placed
on
Mateo's
chest.

SUNRISE FILLS
THE MEADOW

My eyes
shut tight.

Sunrays
on my skin
are warmer
than a bath.

Drenched
in sunlight,
I feel the
source of all
living beings.

Then—

A HEARTBEAT

echoes
into
my
jaw.

Coming
from
Mateo's
chest.

I sit up.

Rodolfo's
solar power beads
on Mateo's
coral necklace
glow white.

They're
feeding on
sunlight.

Mateo
gasps
for air.

His
earthy
eyes
open.

WANT TO KEEP READING?

If you liked this book, check out another
book from West 44 Books:
LIKE WATER FOR DRAGONS
BY MAIJA BARNETT

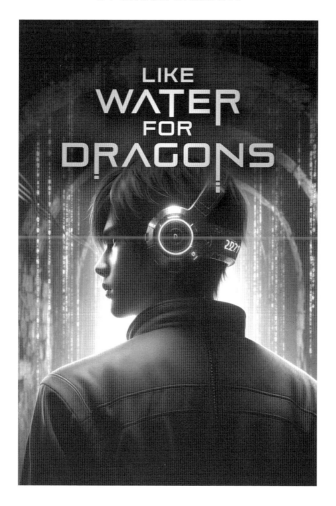

ISBN: 9781978597662

WHAT I REMEMBER

I remember the
sunrise.

My mother's
smile.

Dark hair
flowing
down her back
like
water.

Eyes the color of the sky,
like mine.

I remember our meals.
The coarse brown bread.

Milk straight from the
village goats.

We shared everything,
we people
in hiding.

All of us working
to stay alive.
And away from the war
churning around us.

Away from the creatures
our race
        built.

We didn't have much,
but we had the horizon.

Bright and clear
as a song.

And we still had the stars
staring down from the
darkness.

We still had the parts
that made us
        free.

ME

C-235 is my official name.
But everyone calls me C.

I'm 17, which isn't
good.

(Though with my skinny build,
I look around 12.)

But 18 is the age
you're finished here.

That's when you're
considered
        grown.

When they hack up
your body.

Use it for parts.

Like an old car,
even though you're not
        old.

Even though your life's
just begun.

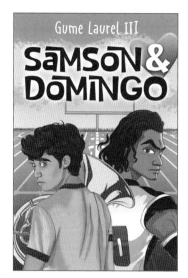

CHECK OUT MORE BOOKS AT:
www.west44books.com

WEST **44** BOOKS™

ABOUT THE AUTHOR

Gume is a Texan Chicano, native to the Rio Grande Valley on the southernmost border. For the past decade, he has dedicated himself to crafting literary works that promote inclusion and showcase diverse characters with intersectional identities. The bulk of Gume's writings are focused on underrepresented groups, especially those from the communities he is a part of: Latine and queer. Gume's other verse novels for West 44 Books are *Samson & Domingo* and *The Brujos of Borderland High*. When Gume isn't writing, he can be found getting lost on a hiking trail with his dogs Blu and Mouse. For more info on what he's up to, check out GumeLaurel.com and @TX.Author on socials.